To: ....

From: ....

Date: ....

REMY THE RHINO
Learns Patience

By
Andy McGuire

HARVEST HOUSE PUBLISHERS

EUGENE, OREGON

For my wife, Becky,
a wonderful model of patience

Remy the Rhino Learns Patience

Copyright © 2010 by Andy McGuire

Published by Harvest House Publishers
Eugene, Oregon 97402
www.harvesthousepublishers.com

ISBN 978-0-7369-2773-4

Artwork © Andy McGuire and published in association with the Books & Such Literary Agency,
52 Mission Circle, Suite 122, PMB 170, Santa Rosa, CA 95409-5370, www.booksandsuch.biz.

Design and production by Franke Design and Illustration, Minneapolis, Minnesota

Printed in China

10 11 12 13 14 15 16 / LP / 10 9 8 7 6 5 4 3 2 1

He'd taken deep breaths and had counted to ten,
But Remy the rhino was charging again.

The zebras, this time, were about to get hurt
'Cause they'd eaten the grass that he'd saved for dessert.
It seemed there was constantly someone to charge
(Because that's what you do when you're angry and large).

His doctor would say he had issues with rage
While his daddy just told him to "Please act your age!"

Everything always made Remy upset:

The dust was too DRY,
the water too WET,

He hated the HEAT and he hated the COLD,
He wouldn't put up with the YOUNG or the OLD,

The meerkats were JUMPY,
the hornbills too LOUD,

Giraffes made him GRUMPY,
the lions too PROUD,

Gazelles were too TIMID,
baboons made him SCOWL,

They'd better stop bothering Remy

RIGHT NOW!!!

One evening he dropped for a snooze on the ground
When an aardvark came bumbling and shuffling around.

Hungry for insects, she searched with her nose
'Til she tripped on a patch of rhinoceros toes.

Well, Remy got mad, as you probably guessed,
But the aardvark did something I wouldn't suggest.
She stood there and waited for Remy to charge her.
She stood there and watched him get closer and **LARGER!**

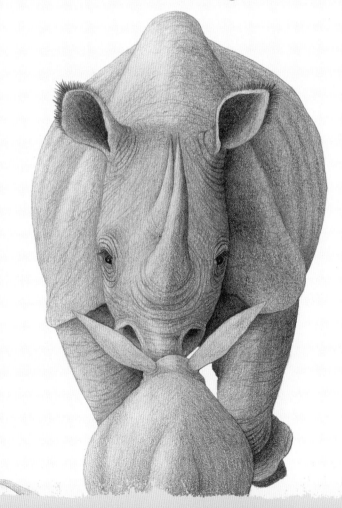

At the very last moment, as quick as can be,
She dodged, and Remy ran into a tree.

He tried to step back, but his horn had got caught,
And the more Remy struggled, the stucker it got.
He groaned and he steamed, he moaned and he grunted,
But still that old tree wouldn't do what he wanted.

He screamed like a banshee, he stomped on the ground.
It sounded like thunder for miles around.
Hundreds of animals fled in confusion,

Then the aardvark said softly,
"I have a solution."

Remy calmed down for a moment or two,
So the aardvark went on, "I know just what to do!
What you need is some creatures to chew on this tree.
I've got some connections; you leave it to me."

The aardvark left Remy alone to consider
What kind of beasts nibbled trees for their dinner.

Remy was growing a little afraid
When the aardvark came back with a termite parade.
"My termites are perfect for work of this kind,
But there's one little thing that you must keep in mind.
Whenever you angrily struggle and jerk,
It scares off the termites and slows down their work."

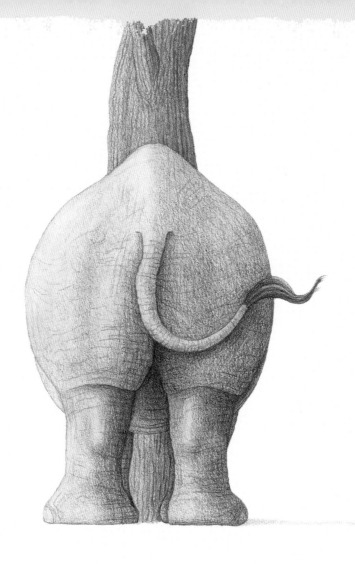

So as Remy experienced strange new sensations,
He took a crash course in the virtue of patience.

He waited through rain and he waited through thunder.

He waited through birds climbing over and under.

He waited through leopards' absurd decorations.

He waited through gawkers from faraway nations.

He waited through elephant balancing acts.

Until little

By little

He learned

To relax.